Welcome to the Family,
Avalene!
We love you!
Love,
Uncle Wesley & Aunt Sarah
Tyler, Devin, & Caleb

Baby Shower Nov. 27, 2010

I Love You So....

by
Marianne Richmond

I Love You So...

LCCN 2004115278

Marianne Richmond Studios, Inc.
3900 Stinson Boulevard NE
Minneapolis, MN 55421
www.mariannerichmond.com

ISBN 10: 1-934082-07-4
ISBN 13: 978-1-934082-07-2

Illustrations by Marianne Richmond

Book design by Sara Dare Biscan

Printed by Cimarron
Minneapolis, MN, USA
Seventh Printing, December 2009

I Love You So...

is dedicated to

Cole James, Adam Jon, Julia Rose, and Will David,
who fill my heart with gigantic love. — MR

I love you as BRILLIANT
as each sparkling star,
and as WAY OUT as space,
I love you THAT far.

I love you as GIGANTIC
as a great lion's roar,
and as DEEP as the ocean,
I love you MUCH more.

YOU put it there, really,
when you and I met.
And I knew for certain
WITHOUT you I'd fret.

From MY HEAD to my TOES,
I was feeling inside
a devotion for you
SO DEEP and SO WIDE.

And now it's ENORMOUS
and wonderfully real
and hard to describe
HOW MUCH I feel!

I love you as AWESOME
as a thundery sky,
and as SOARING as mountains,
I love you THAT high.

I love you as SILLY
as a puppy dog's kiss,
and as QUIET as midnight,
I love you like THIS.

"Do you love me EVERY day?"
you ask with doubting awe,
"or does love go UP 'N DOWN
like a teetering see-saw?"

I love you as STEADY
as the earth rounds the sun,
though SOME days of life
are the FARTHEST from fun.

"Like when you feel MAD?"
      you ask with distress,
"'cause I've BROKEN the rules
      or made a BIG mess?

Or, when I'm UNKIND,
      and your feelings are BLUE,
do you love me ALTHOUGH
      I do what I do?"

I love you being NICE,
and when you're CRANKY, too.
I love you without liking
the NAUGHTY things you do.

My 'love you' DOESN'T change
like the temper of the days.
It's a CERTAIN kind of thing
in many DIFFERENT ways.

You're my SWEETIE, my dear,
my SMILE and laughter.

You're my PLAYMATE for always,
and my JOY ever after.

Hanging out WITH YOU
is where I want to be...
eating ice cream sundaes
or watching the TV.

UNDER your umbrella,
behind you on a bike.
BY you and BESIDE you
is what I REALLY like.

I love you NEAR or FAR.
I love you HIGH or LOW.
My love is there with you
WHEREVER you may go.

"Even when I'm SICK...
    and I can't get out of bed?
Do you love me better HEALTHY
    than with fever in my head?"

I love you sick or able.
You're ALWAYS you to me,
the ONE I LOVE forevermore.
Undeniably.

I CAN'T IMAGINE life
before YOU came along...
me there singing senseless,
no MEANING to my song.

Call it MEANT TO BE
or simply blessed fate,
you fill my heart WITH LOVE...
and for THAT I celebrate.

"WAY, WAY MORE than you know..."